A HOME for a PRINCESS

A Peek Inside
9 Disney PRINCESS Castles

Illustrated by the
Disney Storybook Art Team

Random House New York

Royal Composer
Sebastian is in charge of all the royal concerts.

Head Chef
He does all the cooking at the palace!

Servants
They keep the palace clean and serve everyone who lives here.

Merguards
They protect my family and the palace.

Governess
She is in charge of the education of my sisters and me.

Royal Gardener
He tends the palace gardens.

Royal Butlers
They see to the needs of the palace's guests.

Royal Announcer
He makes all the official palace announcements and lets everyone know when my dad is entering a room. It's a big deal!

Ariel's Vanity Room

My sisters and I use this room to prepare for performances and to relax! We get ready using the reflective surfaces while spending time together and helping each other accessorize. Here we're almost at the top of the palace, so some sunlight makes its way in and allows underwater plants to thrive!

My sister Arista likes to make us laugh—even our oldest sister, Attina!

Flounder loves relaxing with me here!

The fish help us with jewelry! This one is bringing a necklace.

Merida's Castle

I grew up in Castle DunBroch. It stands on the top of a cliff, and its high stone walls have protected my family for centuries. The walls sometimes make me feel a little trapped, though, so I try to get out and explore whenever I can.

Come and take a look around!

Attic

Tapestry Room

My Bedroom

Stairwell
It's easy to get lost here!

Armory

Castle Entrance

Great Hall
This is where we host guests. It can get very noisy when another clan comes to visit!

Mum and Dad's Bedroom

Music Room

Triplets' Bedroom
This is where my three crazy brothers sleep!

Kitchen
This is where I made the cake that turned my mother into a bear. I haven't baked much since then.

Common Room
I love spending time with my family here.

WHO LIVES at the CASTLE?

King Fergus
He's my father and the King of DunBroch.

Queen Elinor
My mother is a wise and elegant queen.

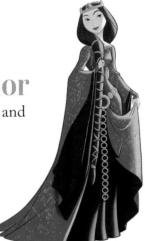

Princess Merida
I'm a princess—but I usually don't feel like one.

Princes Harris, Hubert, and Hamish
They are my triplet brothers. They love sweets and getting into trouble!

Angus
He's my horse and my best friend.

Mama Bear

My mother and I went on an adventure that involved her transforming into a bear—and back into herself again!

Triplet Bears

The curse that turned my mother into a bear also temporarily turned my three brothers into bear cubs!

Maudie

She's the nursemaid who used to take care of me. Now she takes care of my brothers.

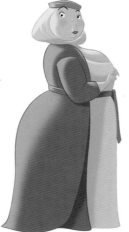

Castle Staff

My mother is in charge of the staff who clean the castle and keep things running.

Cook

Aileen cooks for our family and for guests who come to the castle.

Guards

Gordon and Martin guard the front gate.

This is our family
tapestry, made by
my mum.

This is my tapestry!

We keep lots of colored
thread ready to use.

Mum and I like to
spend time together here,
sipping hot tea by the fire.

The Tapestry Room

My mum spends a lot of time in the Tapestry Room, where she embroiders tapestries that tell our family history. This used to be my least-favorite place in the castle. I thought history and tapestries were SO BORING! But I've learned that our family story is important—and I've even started a tapestry of my own.

Aurora's Castle

Welcome to my castle! I was born here but raised in a cottage in the forest. Now I'm so happy to be back in my family home. I can't wait to show you around!

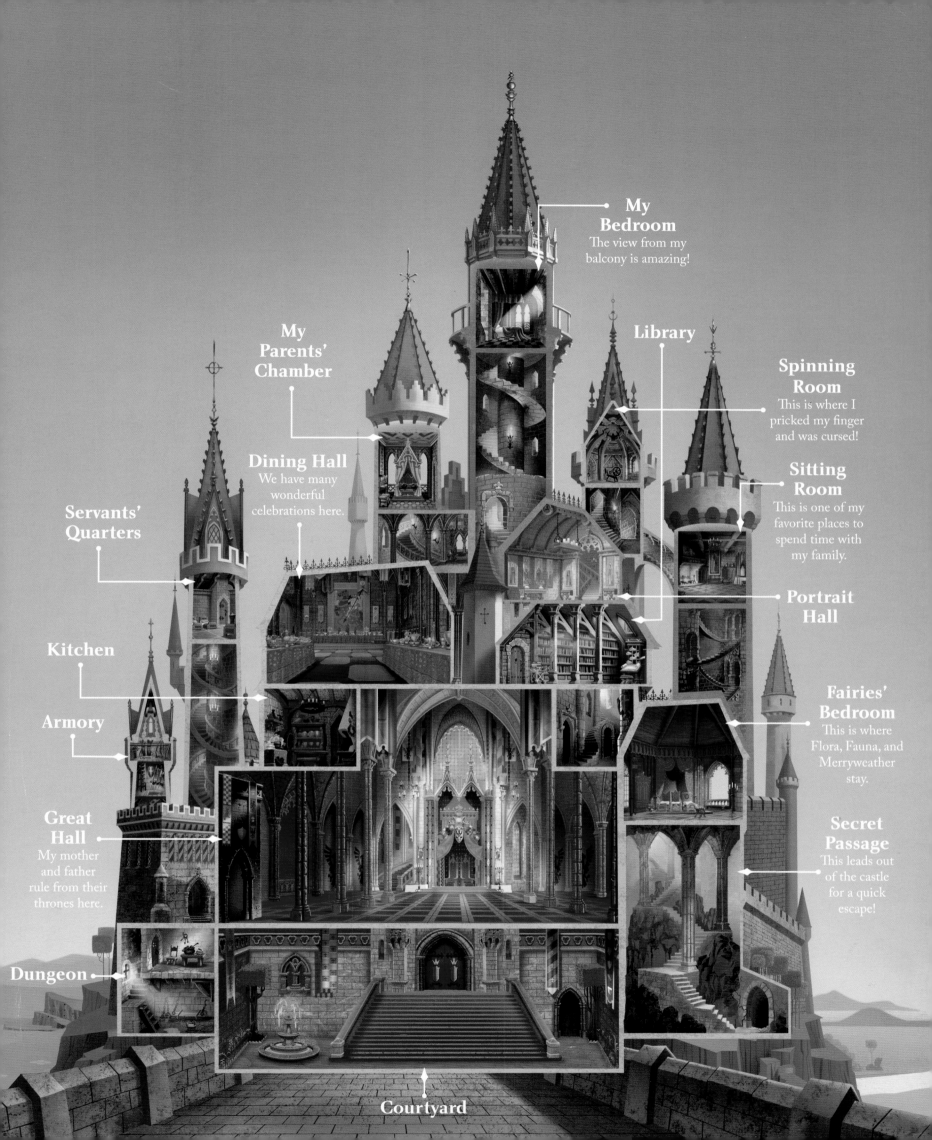

My Bedroom
The view from my balcony is amazing!

My Parents' Chamber

Library

Spinning Room
This is where I pricked my finger and was cursed!

Dining Hall
We have many wonderful celebrations here.

Sitting Room
This is one of my favorite places to spend time with my family.

Servants' Quarters

Portrait Hall

Kitchen

Fairies' Bedroom
This is where Flora, Fauna, and Merryweather stay.

Armory

Great Hall
My mother and father rule from their thrones here.

Secret Passage
This leads out of the castle for a quick escape!

Dungeon

Courtyard

WHO LIVES at the CASTLE?

King Stefan

He's my father.

The Queen

She's my mother.

Princess Aurora

I lived here as a baby, and I am now back after 16 long years away.

Flora

She's one of my aunts and the head good fairy.

Fauna

She's my sweet but scatterbrained fairy aunt.

Merryweather

She's my feisty, headstrong fairy aunt.

Prince Phillip

He's the prince of the nearest kingdom and my love!

King Hubert

He's Prince Phillip's father.

Knights
They protect the castle.

Maids
They keep the castle clean.

Royal Messenger
He makes royal announcements and speeches.

Musician
He entertains royal guests.

Court Jester
He keeps my family and our guests laughing.

Guards
They stand watch at the castle gates.

Trumpeter
He announces the royal family when we arrive.

The Sitting Room

My parents and I gather around the fireplace and spend time together in this cozy private room. This room does not hold only happy memories, though. The evil Maleficent once snuck into the castle through this fireplace. But now that she's been defeated, we can enjoy the room in peace.

I sat at this vanity when Maleficent found me and enacted her curse.

This chandelier has been here longer than I have!

This crest represents my and Prince Phillip's families' union.

Where there was once only wall, Maleficent created a door!

The corner fireplace and cozy blankets keep us warm.

Scullery Maid

Francine helps keep the dishes clean and in good condition.

Waiters

They're in charge of serving food in the dining room.

Wigmaker

Chloe makes wigs for the castle's staff and residents.

Housemaid

Fifi is in charge of cleaning the castle.

House Steward

Molière manages the castle's money.

Knight

Aleron the knight protects the royal family.

Footman

Enzo assists Cogsworth in running the house.

Maestro

Louis's elegant music entertains the castle's residents and guests.

Royal Duster

Demir keeps the castle dust-free!

Valet

Peppy makes sure the castle's guests always look their best.

Guard Dog

He's a sweet and loyal pup.

Chef Bouche does all the cooking.

Magical dishes wash themselves!

These two keep the kitchen clean and tidy!

Chip sleeps in the cupboard with the other teacups.

Mrs. Potts is in charge of everything that happens in the castle's kitchen.

The Kitchen

The castle's kitchen is always a busy place. There is never much time before the next meal, so cooking takes all day, even with a magical stove. But this also means there are always delicious treats for the taking!

Belle's Library

The library is my absolute favorite room in the whole castle! It has every kind of book, and staircases to reach the highest shelves. For a room with so many words, this gift from the Beast left me speechless.

The bookshelves go as high as the ceiling!

I have a grand writing desk where I write stories of my own.

I love sitting by the
cozy fireplace and
reading.

The Beast helps keep our book
collection organized so we
can find everything!

Cinderella's Palace

Welcome to my palace! It's where all my dreams have come true. There are so many beautiful rooms, it's hard to pick my favorite!

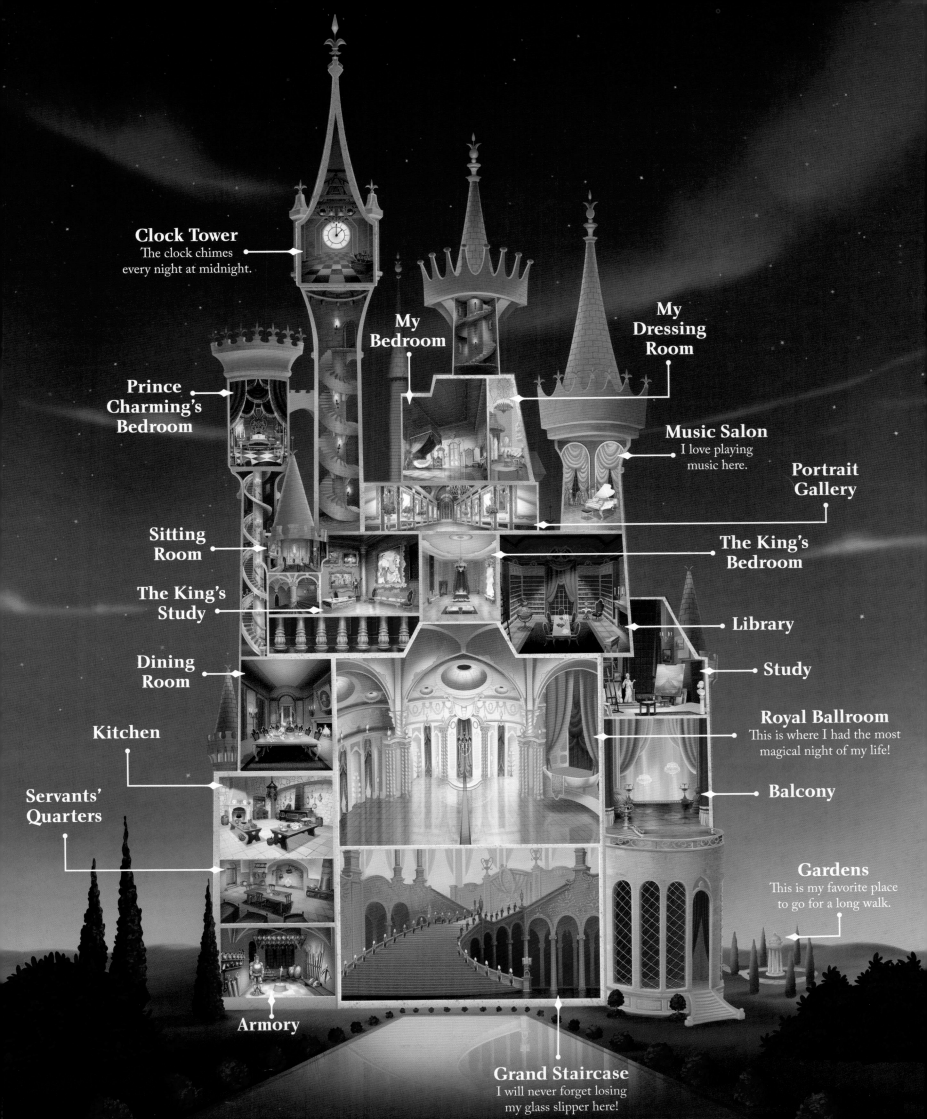

Clock Tower
The clock chimes every night at midnight.

My Bedroom

My Dressing Room

Prince Charming's Bedroom

Music Salon
I love playing music here.

Portrait Gallery

Sitting Room

The King's Bedroom

The King's Study

Library

Study

Dining Room

Royal Ballroom
This is where I had the most magical night of my life!

Kitchen

Balcony

Servants' Quarters

Gardens
This is my favorite place to go for a long walk.

Armory

Grand Staircase
I will never forget losing my glass slipper here!

WHO LIVES at the PALACE?

Princess Cinderella

I still can't believe I get to live in such an amazing palace!

Prince Charming

He has many royal duties, but he always makes time for me.

The King

He rules the kingdom and has been very welcoming to me.

Grand Duke

He helps run the kingdom.

Governess

She teaches the palace children.

Royal Messenger

He delivers messages to and from the palace.

Royal Soldiers

They protect the royal family.

Maestro

He is in charge of
the music for
royal events.

Royal Announcer

He makes all
the important
announcements.

Royal Butlers

They take care of
everything in the
castle, from the pantry
to the bedrooms.

Maids

They keep the
palace neat
and clean.

Knights

They guard
the palace.

Cook

He makes
delicious meals!

Royal Carriage Driver

He drives the magnificent
royal carriage.

I keep trinkets and accessories in these boxes.

I use this dressmaker's dummy to create new outfits.

I have a closet full of gowns!

I use this sketchbook to draw new designs.

Cinderella's Dressing Room

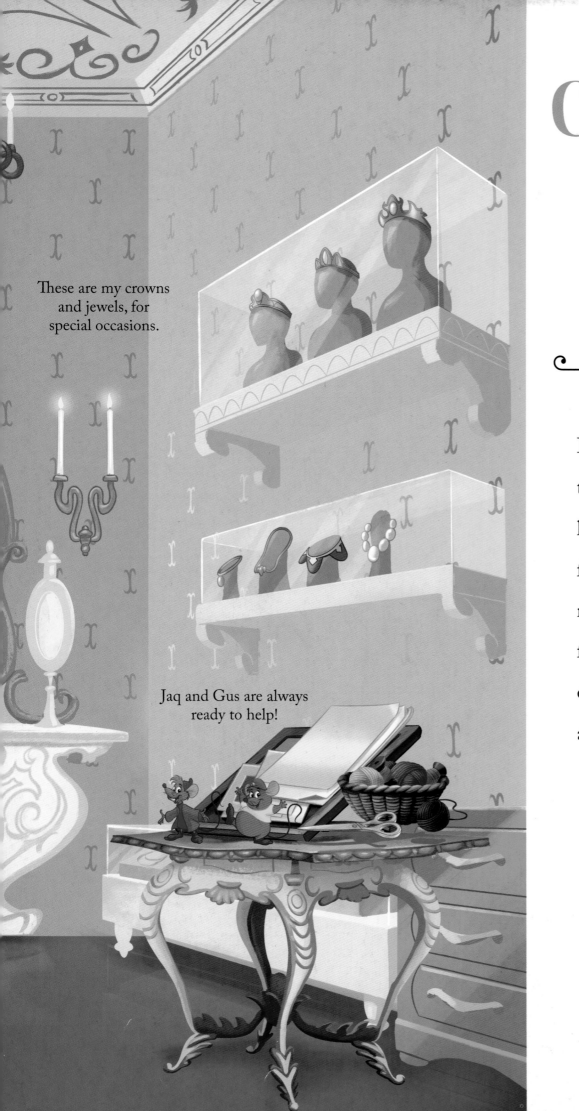

These are my crowns and jewels, for special occasions.

Jaq and Gus are always ready to help!

I have a special dressing room all to myself. I get ready for the day here with the help of my mouse friends. There are lots of mirrors to make sure everything looks perfect from all angles. And there are lots of places for tiaras and jewels, hats and gloves, and of course, dresses!

Mulan
and the
Imperial
Palace

❦ ———————————— ❦

Welcome to the Imperial Palace!
It's the grandest home in all of China.
The Emperor and his family live here, and
it is used to host special guests—like me!

Common Room

Music Room

Tea Room

Red symbolizes
good fortune
and happiness.

**Imperial
Theater**

Imperial Study   **War Room**   **Throne Room**

Emperor's Chamber

Hallway

Balcony

The dragon is the
symbol of the
Emperor.

I once climbed
these columns to
save the Emperor.

WHO is at the PALACE?

The Emperor
He is the wise and kind ruler of China.

Mulan
While I declined the offer to join the Emperor's council, I still visit the palace often to offer my advice.

General Li
This is a brave warrior who once commanded the Imperial Army.

Li Shang
He is General Li's son, who is in charge of army training.

Chi Fu
He is the Emperor's loyal advisor.

Ling
He is a soldier with a great sense of humor.

Yao
We joined the army together and eventually became friends.

Chien-Po
He is a skilled warrior who prefers to resolve problems peacefully.

Drummer

The palace drummer plays at special celebrations and events.

Pi-Pa Player

A pi-pa is a special instrument that's played throughout the palace for family time and celebrations.

Court Lady

Her most important royal duty is making silk that is used for royal clothing and traded around the world.

Acrobat

He performs amazing feats at palace events.

Court Dancer

She entertains royals and guests at festivals and special events.

Family Dog

Little Brother is my sweet, loyal dog.

Mother

My mother wants what's best for me and supports my role in service to the Emperor.

Lucky Cricket

Cri-Kee brings me luck everywhere I go.

Father

I volunteered to join the Imperial Army in order to take my father's place.

Guardian

Mushu is a mighty dragon and my family's guardian.

The Imperial Theater

There is a theater in the palace where the Emperor and his guests can enjoy tea and watch stories told by shadow puppets. These shadow plays are often theatrical retellings of stories that are made famous throughout China! The shadow puppets in this play might look familiar.

Visitors sit on these comfy pillows.

Paper lanterns provide light.

Is that dragon puppet supposed to be Mushu?

There are always tea and treats to enjoy.

Jasmine's Palace

I live in a majestic golden palace in Agrabah. I used to feel trapped here, but now I'm able to venture beyond the walls. Let me show you around!

WHO LIVES at the PALACE?

The Sultan
My father is the Sultan of Agrabah. He is a wise and devoted ruler.

Princess Jasmine
I grew up in the palace; now I help my father run the kingdom.

Aladdin
I'm so glad Aladdin now lives in the palace. He never gets tired of exploring!

Abu
Aladdin's playful monkey keeps everyone entertained.

The Magic Carpet
Carpet loves to zoom through the palace halls!

Rajah
He's my beloved tiger and best friend, and he has lived in the palace with me since he was just a cub.

The Genie
He's usually off exploring the world, but he enjoys spending time at the palace between trips.

Captain of the Guard

Along with the other guards, Rasoul patrols the royal grounds.

Royal Vizier

The evil Jafar used to live in the palace and advise my father, but now he's trapped in a magic lamp.

Iago

Jafar's parrot used to spy on everyone in the palace, but now he's trapped with Jafar in a lamp.

The Cooks

A team of cooks lives in the palace, keeping it full of delicious food.

Imperial Guard

This is an elite group of soldiers who protect the royal family and defend Agrabah.

Governess

She has been my teacher since I was a little girl.

Lady's Maid

She's an expert seamstress who helps me get ready for royal events.

Palace Servants

Many servants keep the palace running every day.

The Throne Room

My father, the Sultan, greets guests in the enormous Throne Room at the center of our palace. Visitors often bring delectable dishes and entertainment to make a good impression, and our décor and hospitality delight in exchange! This is where my father first met Aladdin as Prince Ali!

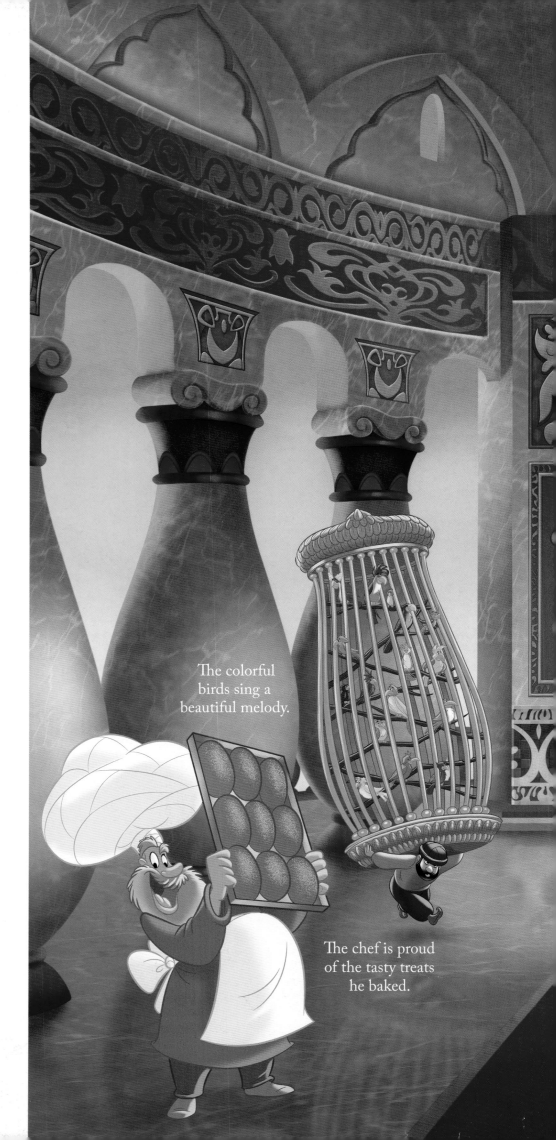

The colorful birds sing a beautiful melody.

The chef is proud of the tasty treats he baked.

The Sultan
sits on this golden
elephant throne,
perfect for a wise leader!

This man
is carrying a
platter while
walking on stilts!
Now, *that's*
impressive.

I used to daydream about the world outside the palace walls while sitting at this window.

Rajah enjoys taking a cozy catnap in here.

Lots of fluffy pillows mean Rajah and I can get comfy!

Sipping hot tea helps me relax.

Soft carpets feel nice on our feet.

The Pillow Room

Our comfortable and colorful Pillow Room is one of my favorite spots in the whole palace. I love relaxing here with Rajah, especially if it is too hot to sit in the garden.

Snow White's Castle

Welcome to my castle! It's been my home since I was a little girl, but the Queen made it less than welcoming during the time she was there. Now I live happily ever after as a princess again. Explore it with me!

Treasure Room

Library

The Queen's Bedroom
She would spy on people through these windows.

Sitting Room

Guest Room

Music Room

Portrait Gallery

The Queen's Chambers

Garderobe
This is a fancy name for a bathroom.

My Bedroom

Hallway

Wishing Well
This is my favorite place in the castle. It's where I wished every day that all my dreams would come true. They did!

Buttery
This is where food and drinks are stored.

Armory

Servants' Quarters

Kitchen

Throne Room

Courtyard

Dungeon
This is where the Queen secretly mixed an evil potion.

❧ WHO is at the CASTLE? ❧

The Queen

She was a cruel ruler and my evil stepmother, with many secrets in the castle. Thankfully, she no longer lives here.

Princess Snow White

My father was the king, but my stepmother, the Queen, never treated me as a princess.

The Prince

He lives in a nearby kingdom and made it his mission to help me.

Huntsman

He works for the castle and saved me from the evil Queen.

Messenger

He delivers messages to and from the Queen.

Cook

He's in charge of feeding everyone in the castle.

Maids

The maids make sure the castle stays neat and clean.

Knights

The knights are brave and loyal defenders of the castle.

The Miners

The Seven Dwarfs were responsible for mining the nearby hills for diamonds for the Queen.

Butler

He's in charge of keeping the castle stocked with food and drinks.

Musicians

They keep the castle filled with beautiful music.

Juggler

He keeps everyone in the castle entertained with his crazy skills.

Acrobats

They provide entertainment for everyone in the castle.

The Witch

This was really the Queen in disguise!

Watchman

He patrols the castle when everyone else has gone to bed.

The Queen's Chambers

These were the Queen's private rooms, where she kept her Magic Mirror and other secret items. The Queen would visit the Magic Mirror every morning. The spirit trapped inside the Magic Mirror could only tell the truth.

Peacocks represent the Queen's powers.

Zodiac, or star, symbols frame the mirror.

These curtains hid the Magic Mirror when the Queen was not using it.

The Magic Mirror is really a spirit trapped inside a piece of glass.

This is a box for hiding secrets.

Rapunzel's Castle

I'm so glad you've come to visit my castle! My family has lived here for many generations, and I'm happy to call this amazing place my home again.

Attic
Those are my paintings on the dome walls.

Astrology Room
This is the best place for stargazing.

Bell Tower

My Art Studio

My Bedroom

My Parents' Chambers

Eugene's Bedroom

Throne Room

The Statue Hall

Hall of Portraits

Soldiers' Quarters

Dining Room

Armory

Pantry

Dungeon

Kitchen

Royal Entrance

Terrace
This is where lanterns are released on my birthday every year.

Stables

WHO LIVES at the CASTLE?

King Frederic

My father is a kind and loyal king.

Queen Arianna

My mother led a very adventurous life before she became queen. Now she always has the best advice!

Princess Rapunzel

That's me! I'm finally back home in the kingdom of Corona after being kidnapped as a baby.

Eugene Fitzherbert

Once a thief called Flynn Rider, Eugene now lives in the castle and helps out however he can.

Maximus

A member of the royal guard, he is a strong and loyal friend.

Pascal

He is a chameleon and my best friend. We do everything together!

Jester

He entertains the royal household, especially when we have guests!

Priest

He is a teacher and leader of church services in the castle.

Head Cook

He oversees all the kitchen staff in the castle.

Captain of the Guard

He's the leader of the royal guard and in charge of keeping the castle safe.

Personal Guard

He keeps watch at my door day and night (but I've figured out how to sneak past him).

Royal Guard

The royal guard protects and castle and the entire kingdom.

Musicians

They keep the guests entertained at royal celebrations.

Governess

She's a teacher for the children of the castle, and she's also been teaching me etiquette.

Housemaids

They make sure things run smoothly and stay tidy in the castle.

This is a portrait of Maximus.

Pascal strikes a pose for me.

I read all these books while I was trapped in the tower.

I play my guitar when I need a break from painting.

Rapunzel's Art Studio

I love having my very own art studio! I can play guitar, and read, and obviously paint—and I love to paint portraits of my friends and family! I spend a lot of time here working on my art. Check out my latest masterpiece!

rhcbooks.com
ISBN 978-0-7364-4024-0
MANUFACTURED IN CHINA
10 9 8 7 6 5 4 3 2 1

Random House Children's Books supports the First Amendment and celebrates the right to read.